Tulsa goes to the Ball

There are lots of Early Reader stories
you might enjoy.

Look at the back of the book or,
for a complete list, visit
www.orionbooks.co.uk

Tulsa goes to the Ball

Written and illustrated by
Tony Ross

Orion
Children's Books

First published in Great Britain in 2015
by Orion Children's Books
a division of Hachette Children's Group
and published by Hodder & Stoughton

Orion House
5 Upper Saint Martin's Lane
London WC2H 9EA
An Hachette UK Company

1 3 5 7 9 10 8 6 4 2

Text and illustrations © Tony Ross 2015

The moral right of Tony Ross to be identified
as author and illustrator of this work has been asserted.

The paper and board used in this paperback are natural and recyclable
products made from wood grown in sustainable forests.
The manufacturing processes conform to the environmental
regulations of the country of origin.

ISBN 978 1 4440 1248 4

A catalogue record for this book is available from the British Library.

Printed and bound in China

www.orionchildrensbooks.co.uk

"Tulsa, you **mucky** pup!"
Mum said.

"Have you **seen** the state of your bedroom? It looks as if the seven dwarves, the three bears, **and** the forty thieves had a party in there.

It's a **mess**! Clean it up please."

Tulsa frowned. Only this morning, Mum had asked her to have a bath, and then, on top of that, told her to clean her teeth!

She snorted, "I have to do **everything** around here."

Tulsa stamped up the stairs. She stamped as loudly as she could, so that everyone could hear that she was doing what she was told.

Looking round her room,
Tulsa couldn't see what all the
fuss was about. The room looked
perfectly tidy to her.

It always looked like this,
and she knew exactly where
everything was.

Tulsa banged about for a few
minutes, so the noise would make
Mum think that she actually **was**
doing some tidying.

Then she flung herself onto her bed, and chose a book from the ones she kept under her pillow.

"Just right for me!" she said out loud.

"Why?" said a squeaky voice from her clean pants drawer.

The voice belonged to Tulsa's talking frog. The frog was one of those frogs, who when kissed, would turn into a handsome prince.

The thing was, Tulsa didn't like the idea of kissing a frog.

"**Why** is that book just right
for you?" insisted the frog.

"Because it is about a girl who
has to do all the work around the
house, just like me!

That's why she is called
Cinderella, because she has to
clean out all the cinders."

"Really?" said the frog.

"Yes, really." said Tulsa. "I'm **just** like Cinderella. From now on, you can call me Cindy."

"OK, Cindy, give us a kiss, and I'll be your handsome prince."

"Errr, not yet," said Cindy, who liked the idea of having a pet with good conversation.

"I'd like you to do something for me first."

"And what might that be?" said the frog.

"Have you ever read
Cinderella?" asked Tulsa.

"No," replied the frog. "Until I
met you, I lived in a pond. I might
be able to talk, but I can't read."

"Well, Cinderella is about a girl
who has to do all the work, and
her ugly sisters did nothing at all.

While Cinderella was doing
all the work, the ugly sisters were
invited to a wonderful ball, thrown
by a handsome prince."

"That sounds like me," said the
frog.

"Anyway, Cinderella couldn't
go to the ball, because of all the
washing up, and then she had to
tidy her room.

The prince was upset, because he really wanted to dance with Cinderella."

"Gosh!" said the frog.

"Then along came a fairy godmother, who fixed it so Cinderella could go to the ball. She changed her rags into a beautiful dress, a pumpkin into a carriage, and mice into horses."

"How?" breathed the frog.

"Because she was enchanted."

"Like me!" squealed the frog.

"Exactly like you," said Tulsa, nodding.

"Where is all this leading?" muttered the frog.

"Well," said Tulsa, "I want you to take me to the ball!"

"What ball?" said the frog.

"The **enchanted** ball," said Tulsa.

"I don't know what you are talking about," said the frog.

"But you are an enchanted
frog. You **should** know what
to do!" snapped Tulsa. "It's easy,
you get a pumpkin, or I suppose
any vegetable would do, and you
change it into a beautiful coach."

The frog blinked.

"Then," went on Tulsa, "you change yourself into a fine white pony and take me to the ball."

"I can't do that!" gasped the frog. "If I could change myself into things, I would have turned into a handsome prince years ago."

"Then," Tulsa went on, "you must change my jeans and top into a wonderful ball gown."

"I'm a FROG!" said the frog, "I can talk, but mainly I croak, and swim. I will jump for you if you like, but I can't do all those other things."

"I'm Cindy," said Tulsa, "and you are a magic frog. Take me to the ball."

The frog knew that there was no point in arguing. He thought for a moment, then said sadly, "Alright, I will take you to the ball. You will have to pretend the coach and all that, and I can't do anything about the dress."

"OK," said Tulsa. "I will go as I am."

She burrowed in her pocket and pulled out a pink ribbon, and tied it round the frog's neck."

"What do you think you are doing?" squeaked the frog.

"I am pretending you are a fine white pony, and I am in a coach, and I am wearing a beautiful gown." said Tulsa. "Giddy up! Take me to the ball."

The frog hopped out of Tulsa's room, and down the stairs, through the kitchen and out into the garden.

The royal coach had to stop,
while Tulsa opened the gate onto
the lane.

As they went down the lane,
Tulsa waved to cheering crowds,
and the frog did his best to be a
fine white pony.

The coach jumped over the stile, and around the cornfield. The pony stopped to catch his breath by the church.

"Are we nearly there?" said Tulsa. She was getting excited now. The frog **did** know the way to the enchanted ball.

"Not far now," wheezed the frog,
heading for a little clump of trees.

He came to a halt by a pond.
It was the pond that he was born
in, the pond where he used to live,
before the clean pants drawer.

"Why have we stopped here?"
asked Tulsa.

"Why, Your Majesty, Princess
Cindy, we are at the ball!" said the
frog, proudly.

Tulsa looked around in amazement. "I can't see any ball," she said.

"There!" squealed the frog, pointing to the edge of the pond. "There's your ball."

Tulsa blinked. Bobbing about
in the rushes, was the old football
that she had lost in the spring.
There it was, her favourite ball.

She grabbed it, and dried it off
on her tee shirt. She danced about,
hugging it.

"My very best ball, from Uncle Alan!" she cooed happily, "I wondered where **that** was!"

"It's the only ball I know about," said the frog.

"Now, how about a kiss?"

What are you going to read next?

Have more adventures with
Horrid Henry,

or save the day with Anthony Ant!

Become a
superhero with Monstar,

float off to
sea with
Algy,

or have your very own Pirates' Picnic.

Grow carrots with

Lottie and Dottie,

make magic with The Witch Dog,

and cast a spell with

The Three Little Magicians.

Enjoy all the Early Readers.